Letters from Cody

A Young Fentanyl Victim's Letters
to His Mom from Heaven

ARIANE EYA

BALBOA.PRESS

A DIVISION OF HAY HOUSE

Balboa Press books may be ordered through booksellers or by contacting:

Balboa Press
A Division of Hay House
1663 Liberty Drive
Bloomington, IN 47403
www.balboapress.com
1 (877) 407-4847

Because of the dynamic nature of the Internet, any web addresses or links contained in this book may have changed since publication and may no longer be valid. The views expressed in this work are solely those of the author and do not necessarily reflect the views of the publisher, and the publisher hereby disclaims any responsibility for them.

The author of this book does not dispense medical advice or prescribe the use of any technique as a form of treatment for physical, emotional, or medical problems without the advice of a physician, either directly or indirectly. The intent of the author is only to offer information of a general nature to help you in your quest for emotional and spiritual well-being. In the event you use any of the information in this book for yourself, which is your constitutional right, the author and the publisher assume no responsibility for your actions.

Any people depicted in stock imagery provided by Getty Images are models, and such images are being used for illustrative purposes only. Certain stock imagery © Getty Images.

Print information available on the last page.

ISBN: 978-1-9822-3762-2 (sc)
ISBN: 978-1-9822-3761-5 (e)

Library of Congress Control Number: 2019917141

Balboa Press rev. date: 11/05/2019

To my son ... my joy, my laughter, and my lifestyle changer ... my dearest child who took some drugs and died so young:
I loved you a lot.

Mom

- The epidemic of drug-induced deaths continues in North America today. Statistics indicate that there are approximately nine deaths per hour (or over 215 deaths each day), related to opioid use, in Canada and the United States combined.

- In the USA and Canada over 350,000 people (including men, women, and young people) have lost their lives to fentanyl and other drug overdoses in the past five years (since 2014). Cody was among these overdose victims; in 2017 fentanyl caused his death.

- According to airline statistics, in the past four years, around 2,900 passengers have died in accidents around the world—or about 725 lives have been lost each year.

- In 2018 alone more than 68,600 people have died due to fentanyl and other drug overdoses in the United States.

May we now, find a solution so that we can all be safe? Let us put aside our shame and fight with confidence to combat this disgraceful epidemic.

Letter 1

Hey, Mommy,

$\mathcal{M}$y name is Cody. I'm in heaven today. I loved you.

PS: I am still the same old Cody, so don't forget this. And send regards to those who don't care, as I don't seek to talk to them too often anymore. As you know, they seemed to have moved on a long time ago, about a year and a half, but you still dream about me, talk to me, and keep me company from earth.

I am still with thee, and you see how much I care!

Mom, don't cry. It makes me sad too, as I am so, so sorry for all I've done. And Jesus says this: "You were a swell mom, all in all."

Think about this. Jesus says it, so it must be right.

Cody,
your son always,
from heaven

Letter 2

Hi, Mom,

I am fine. Don't worry about me. We have always loved each other, you and I. The time we spent is precious to me always, and to you, too, I presume.

If Dad ever says something to hurt you again, I will surely die again to come back to earth as a winged serpent and smash his head against his own dogmas.

But where you've been has been hardest of all, fighting against loveless, sadistic abuse while parenting us—both Maureen (do you appreciate what Mom did, dear sister?) and me—most of the years. The reasons are too plentiful to list right here.

Over the years, you succumbed to abuse but never alcohol or drugs.

Some days you got out of sorts in a way Maureen and I saw, and we truly didn't care to see that at all.

The reasons again were so deep, and this sadistic, evil torment takes you finally out as well as perpetrating my own demise.

The end wasn't good, but it came via a love affair with this yahoo who didn't care shit about anybody else. And now this Claudina enters his life. She has a foul mouth and a badass attitude, and she threw me out on the streets at night. That was saddest event I lived through and died as a result of, in that order. At the end, he knows this well.

This man truly wasn't there for me.

But sister Maureen was also abused by her. These adults tango in a dance of death abusing their kids—and solely for their own benefit.

Too sad it ended somewhat violently in terms of this emotional toll on both.

I love you, Mommy

Cody,
from heaven

Always love me,
Always cherish
memories that aren't sad,
and
don't blame yourself anymore; this devil is to blame, and I loved you to the end.

Always remember this:
Forgiveness is the key
to satisfaction in life.
Forgiveness releases
all the pain inside,
also in me, and I didn't forgive Valeriane,
Dad's wife number two, for abusing me and leaving me outside
this "family" of fear.

𝓑ut I'm forgiving you, and so it's a bigger sadness too. So just forgive my dad, me (Cody), Valeriane, and even Maureen, as at the end, it was you, too, who left me alone to die.

I guess you didn't trust God, as you do now, when He asked you to relieve me from pain and suffering via a small visit.

Bye for now,
Your son,
Cody,
from heaven now

Letter 4

Hi, Mommy,

The lifestyles of evil people have three significances: (a) They yell and scream a lot, (b) they shout and hit people, and (c) they steal! And all that abuse creates a lot of pain. Most people know this, obviously, but they still do it.

Why?

I'm alone and crying myself to sleep, but nobody cares. Where is my family? Why don't they love me anymore?

I questioned myself and concluded I'm not worthy anymore. For some time I tried to understand. Where is this love we had for each other? Where is your family when you need them most? The days were few at the end when I wasn't ill with sadness.

But the days of pain were plenty, for this fighting you did with Dad was surely sadistic and evil and very mean to me and Maureen. And thousands of dollars went down the drain in legal fees and all. Tens of thousands, even. Why? Did you want to win against Dad or something? He's a money expert, and it's truly like tormenting the devil himself.

There is absolutely no need!

God needs none of these people's assistance. He could have saved you on day one, so never do it again. Okay?

Cody

Letter 5

Hi, Mommy,

$\mathcal{I}$ want to talk to you about love today. I died alone, abusing drugs, which is not your fault by the way. I died because you didn't believe.

This has to stop. Right now.

I have a thing or two to say about those prayers you gave me. I prayed but still died alone. Why?

You say you didn't know what to expect, whether I would live or die. My prayer beads are still hanging from the hook by your bed. Why not show them to Dad? They're there to remind you and Maureen that you tried. At least you tried all you could.

Why don't you now make a choice and run with it? Why do you still hesitate to live and to love yourself? Why don't you be the "renegade hero"? I only needed that. You were very sweet, Mommy, but not too brave at the end of it all.

And anyone who knows you, knows you are settled and kind in your ways, but some of us aren't that enlightened yet. So trust in you today, okay? Trust and believe with all your might.

As most seek for answers after I went ahead and took those drugs, many are still contemplating their own role in deaths such as mine.

Sometimes abuse sits right at the core of friendship; sometimes those you trust most betray you at the end. Still, most believe a God can save anybody. But overall, even He can't think of a better way than to sink a dagger into your heart, to purify it from sinister jealousy or any bitterness and envy, than through this way of mine.

So you should thank Him all you can since He sees souls deep.

You needed me to die a sad and angry end so you and Maureen can be redeemed by these wounds on me.

I died alone; you aren't, but you will perhaps want to. So be blessed now. My sweet sister, Maureen. Also you are a sneaky one, always wanting to please, who also put me to my death … and some.

Thousands of people die today due to this fentanyl epidemic, but in truth, they may sometimes want to die at the end as nobody truly has their backs anymore.

(Don't lie to Mommy, Maureen, I beg of you.)

Bye for now, ♥
Cody

Letter 6

Hi, Mom,

$\mathcal{I}$ sit at the pulpit today as I am preaching about love that hasn't been acknowledged yet, the love that I had for you.

The good will cater to others, the good, like you, who ended up paying for all this with your sorrow and pain, those who aren't stingy, but are generous to us, are *truly* generous people.

I had it all wrong all the way, though it's true. What I should have told you is this: "I love you, Mommy, no matter what, and we shall be together all day, long after today even, but not yet forever!"

But I didn't. Instead, I lied. I told you I was planning for college or even a job, but I wasn't. I was suicidal and wanted to leave it all. I now regret this decision, as life has a lot to offer a nineteen-year-old handsome guy like me. So that was sad and wrong of me!

I want you to know that drugs don't make people die; I did it myself. I wanted you to know this: I did drugs, and I decided to die early.

Too early, if you ask me now. I knew all the dangers and took them in stride, without any knowledge of my life actually ending so swiftly and so slowly at the same time.

I thought it was the end of the ends. I had no clue that this is the way: to love somebody so much that your heart is in pain. And this, that you even end up writing a whole book about it after you have died.

I love you, Mommy, I love you. Please do understand that we are together, forever and a day, and that we will never forget each other. Never.

I promise.

And my word was always good.

Cody,
your son
in heaven now and very handsomely so!

Hello,

*M*aureen and I loved each other a bunch. So I thought I'd start with a different tone today, as I am in heaven, you see. When I was a kid and only seven or eight years old, I know you tried. I think you worked so hard that you were pretty exhausted most days, and my dad wasn't pleased at all, because he sees you as a leech on his wealth. But I know you, Mom. You aren't about to flog another human being. You were right and wrong at the same time.

A: So you shall never "steal" again from child support payments and say we need this and then buy yourself a summer lair instead. And a horse!

B: You shall never lie again in court that we needed something as stupid as ski jackets, as you received a large settlement already.

But also, you shall never again be so scolded and abused.

Thank you very much.

I know your heart, Mom, and I know you loved riding and sports (and dad and Valeriane didn't see this so they scorned you), but you do still … and I'm glad you're back at it. And as you got the chance there and took it, isn't so sad, but I also know Dad, and he absolutely *hates* you! … So sorry, but he truly does. So please, Mommy, you don't need to lie, just say this to yourself from now on: "Okay, I did these things, and I am sorry, and Cody and Maureen were okay with it (as I asked them always for permission)."

You can say this, since it's the truth. And we always said yes to you, always …. And sorry, Mommy, for all your pain, and sorry for Dad for being so mean; he is still paying for this, you see …

As I did mean to die in his arms, and not yours.

Bye for now,
Cody

Letter 8

$\mathcal{C}$ody, it's Mom. I'm so sorry … I cried a river (and a half at least …). I wailed and stomped and was in every kind of pain for three years after you left. I am still very keen on making amends; what shall I do?

Mom

———————

Mom! Mom! Do you hear me?

I am here!

I am sitting in your living room! Can you hear me?

I am *very upset! Mom!* Please listen to me from now on!

————————————————

Okay, well … I'll just write these letters instead, because sometimes you aren't around to see me when I want you to. I'll tell you a story about a little man, a very small guy whose name is Sal … yes, *your dad*, Sal. He's from a Nordic country, a "true" Nordic man at heart. I know, I wanted to "punch his lights out," but I never told you this,

He is a "perv." I knew you didn't know this or …

(I think you thought about this but didn't see, choosing to be all about the overall politeness instead).

And yes, he stole your high-heeled shoes from your cabin, the ones with the high and narrow heels, and he stole a number of other objects—from your panties to your dressing gowns. I know this now …

He's truly a pervert!

Did you let him touch me and Maureen?

Why didn't you let us go to parties and soccer? Instead, we always were there, with relatives. Are they your "gods" or something?

Just to "serve" them, you stayed with these old fools, every single weekend. Are you truly *insane* to let this happen to me and Maureen?

I grew to know nothing but abuse as a kid, and he practically fondled Maureen in *plain sight!*

I am *appalled*, Mom. Why didn't you see it?

Now I think I know this: he wanted *me* and Maureen there to be *fondled* and *abused* every single weekend, and you let him!?

Why?

Mom, didn't you see it? Truly say right now. (I know, your answer is one simple and straightforward one, as you didn't know or understand it yourself, since you were abused too by him and her.) I know you didn't even suspect this, as your entire brain forgot every single little act of abuse he inflicted on you *and* your friends even. Every single one was forgotten, vaulted inside, your darkest moments on earth, which you locked up deep inside your mind—and then forgot.

Please now—stay away from that guy from now on, as he's a pervert … he truly is.

Cody,
your son who is in heaven *now*
(due to this "thing" also!).

———-

I am alone …

Help me!

Help, Mommy!

I am so alone …

I don't know where I am …
it's darkness, … and sadness …

I'm dying here …!
…

Letter 9

Mom!

*M*ommy! ... Help!

My mom is sitting and praying her heart out. I know this, as her voice penetrates this darkness: "Cody! Cody!" she yells. "Cody!" She asks me to call on the name of Jesus. "He'll come for you. Trust *Him*. Cody, please trust me. I can't get you back anymore. You need *Him*.

"Cody!"

I stand on the Milky Way as it seems, and slowly turn around, hesitating, and have a very hard time. Suddenly, all I want is for her to be here with me and me to be *back* home and truly *repent* and *be okay!* But now I'm *nowhere*, it seems. In this darkness there's stars, but nothing else. Where am I?

"Cody!"

She's calling through the darkness and prays quietly ...

"Dear Jesus, Lord, go and get him—he's alone!"

Over and over again she prays and prays, for more than two hours, talking to God about me, asking Him to forgive me, her, and everybody and to talk to me so that I understand ....

"Help Cody!"

She cries and asks for mercy for me and also for Him to forgive this son who repents silently inside ... but it's too late for life, and he died.

"Mom!" I exclaim. "Mom, *Mom*, I want to come home. *Now. I want to come to you!*"

I cry alone in the dark empty ... and I am alone. My worst nightmare has come true, as nobody cares anymore about me... Some lights flicker and die, and he's gone.

The end of Cody's life happened on a Monday morning in May, a spring morning with a beautiful breeze, a spring morning here in California, and nobody came for him. He slowly took his last breath, his fingernails turned blue, and his sigh was ever so slight as he passed on.

Letter 10

To: Mommy,

A buse is inside, the hearts and minds of thousands are polluted with the devil's lies.

It doesn't matter where they are; their situation inside or outside the established religions, their native beliefs, or none at all, is irrelevant. The issue is lovelessness, for self and a God higher than us. If nobody cares, it's evil.

If only everyone knew how it is here in heaven, how loving and kind. Nobody would want to live! "That's why we set up barriers for entry," says Jesus to God … and some.

But after three minutes of floating we have a deal, as my mommy is there and prays so hard that Jesus comes for me, and He smiles and says, "Your Mom is a pray-er. She is trying as hard as she can right now and I heard her! So I pray for her too … that she continues to seek for Me and nobody else as a solution from now on." He laughs, and my old long-passed dogs Jo, and also Carla are there! We jump around, and I feel more okay now. I'm with "family" here. So Jesus just takes my arm, and we go on together. I look back, but He is expecting me to follow, and we ascend this small ladder towards a party that seems to be waiting for me …

I am welcome, at last ….

He says, "It's your birthday, Cody (you made it!)."

"What?" I exclaim. "My birthday? I never celebrated on earth. They forgot about me most of the time …," and I smile and shake hands with relatives never met before, but they all are happy to see me! Heaven's gates were slight, just a garland over a gateway, and there's some small meadow as it seems, but there's a nice table set, with cakes and candles for me. "Is this it?"

"It is," says Jesus as He smiles and leads me on. "You did well, son. I'm proud of you."

I smile back and am shy, as usual, and the celebration begins,

We are Home, at last.

Don't cry for me, Mommy.

I was sent to tell you this to get all things straightened out for you and all of you, so be careful. Take care of sister Maureen, and smile at least once in a while already,

Cody,
your *son*
who's in *heaven* now ….

Letter 11

Mom,

True stories here. I was a pretty small kid, until I was about seventeen years old, and I got teased a lot. And I crumbled for the most part.

My name was Cody, but your name, well, wasn't so well liked in your country of origin, as it's unusual, and they teased you, right? I know your name sounded funny to other kids at your school, but you weren't afraid, just really annoyed, and changed to a tough little one because of it.

If only you could have shared some of that mojo with me also, as I always was ashamed of my short stature, and when in front of people, I was shy and mostly afraid, at least a bit. I know this: most days you weren't sure anymore about who you were either, because Dad, his new wife Valeriane, and all these other people were after your mojo, but they lost, didn't they? As I *always* sided with you, didn't I now? …

Also, well before I was born, you loved me. I'll tell you why: because you always loved every sad simple joker in town and tried to help them, so God gave you *me* to deal with, so you get *out of that shit now.* Nobody is ashamed as you are for everything, so let it go now. Let people deal with their *own* issues, and you can just keep going on. Okay?

(I want you to.)

Cody,
the "no-good son"
of yours, with *love*,
who's in heaven now at nineteen years old

Letter 12

Mom,

$\mathcal{S}$ometimes you can strengthen the soul if you can take abuse, but if you grow bitter—as you somewhat did—then it can damage you after a while, inside and out!

Trust me, I know who you are, sometimes a very "bitter old lady"! So never crumble, just be strong! And *laugh* in the face of any abusers, and say, "You are silly. I don't love you *at all*." (That truly is a pissy shit to them.)

Cody (I know)
Cody from heaven
(I know)

Letter 13

Mom,

$\mathcal{S}$orry to pester you again, but you need to have some fun in life, don't you? I think you should. I have an idea: Take yourself to Mexico! And get drunk, and smoke—you used to *love* smoking, so don't you hesitate! (But only in Mexico.) And I am there with you a hundred percent of the way.

Cody, your *only son*
in heaven … *(¡México arriba!)*

Letter 14

Mom,

$\mathcal{T}$oday, and tomorrow, and every single day, please be kind to my sister too, as she isn't too hard on you. (You know she knows all—that in the end you alone were with me, and so on, and this: you would be there now if you could, but not then.)

So please be gentle with her too, as we were the best pals ever. We always talked about everything (you don't know this), and we talked bad stuff about you too, as well as some other jerks, and we told each other secrets and all. So be kind, I beg of you. She's my sister, my ally, and my confidante. Not even you are as close to me as she was! Please be gentle with her, and do take great care of our dogs, especially my Bonney, the sweetest pit bull terrier.

:) from Cody, who was too scared to walk Bonney alone!

… from heaven

Mom,

$\mathcal{H}$ ope you aren't too tired to talk, and hope you listen! I told you about the dealers and how they are. They aren't *nice* at all, to you or others—and from now on, I tell you more: they *think you're their enemy, and they think they are so coolios.* Although I feel they aren't worthy of a note here, I must tell you something else: they blame *me* for dying. They say it's the user's fault, that I did meet my end due to me, not them. They do create death, however.

So why don't you do something about this plague? As in "legalize, standardize, educate, and decriminalize ASAP." Mom, I count on you …

I know they weren't our "friends," but now I know this also: they say they will look after you also while they deal you death in a bag! They are *liars, thieves,* and *murderers* of *children!* That's what they *are!*

These guys are dangerous, so be careful around anyone who isn't your truth and love. These guys at the end gave me this poison that killed me ….

They *killed* and *maimed* me;

they did it.

And at the end they also sold me these drugs with fentanyl, looking to get forty dollars from a small, childish man like me, so to the end a "friend in need" indeed that dealer is!

Cody

Letter 16

Mommy,

$\mathcal{I}$ have a son here now too! I named him after your best dog; his name is Garçon. He's a good boy, and I understand you now much better, your agony. If *anything* happened to my little lad, I would be ready to kill and maim too, and to punish and to punch, and you only watched me take my last … only you knew that I was on my last legs, so to speak, and you did nothing. I am admiring your strength, I would have called the cops …

And I think Dad is insane for letting me go downhill like that in that lair he gave me to live at, but you, why on *earth* didn't you interfere?

I know you had no more energy in you at all after years of fights in court, and three-plus years of 24/7 care of a young suicidal kid; that must be tough. I would have let you go after year one, so don't be sad. I would *never* have given you a *dime* by the way, if it was up to me.

Your *son* Cody,
from *heaven!*

Letter 17

Mommy,

$\mathcal{T}$omorrow is the very last of these letters. Are you sad? I bet …

I am also a bit apprehensive, but ends are ends, and we never can negotiate them … so here goes one of the final ones. I am in heaven. Do you know what it means? I bet you don't, or else you wouldn't be so sad, so I tell you in more detail now,

Heaven is swell. It's so beautiful that, compared to the place, where you sit right now, writing and looking over the Pacific Ocean with whales jumping and eagles soaring, that is a *dive*, and I mean it. I am in heaven, and I can't tell you how much this sucks for me to reminiscence my pitiful stupid choices in life, but I am, since Jesus wanted me to (and He's hard to please), but anyhow …. So heaven is like a bonbon, with sugar on top and sparkles, except clean from anything unhealthy!

Heaven is like a kiss from a maiden with a very nice disposition and a pure heart, and heaven is like an embrace of my mother who was so happy when I came home and just laughed when I wasn't thinking straight. That's what heaven is like, all in one. So would *you* want to trade this for earth? *No!*

I wouldn't come back if I had the chance. Seriously, I would *not come back*. Do you hear me? No way, José. *No!*

Nobody will or would or ever has, because once you are here, you're are *out* of there.

Thank you for telling me about Jesus, since He *rocks*. (PS: He smokes weed ….) Keep at it, Mommy!

Cody, your *son*
in *heaven*
Puff * puff …!

Letter 18

Hi Mom,

*T*alk therapy isn't for me. I wanted you to know this—that I am *not* the kind of guy who talks about me all the time. I think you tried to make me go to therapy, when you could have gone instead!

You know, you talk a lot anyhow, and mostly about you and dad, but a therapist is *paid* to listen; I'm not!

So *stop talking* to your kids. There. Especially about me or *him* entirely, *now!*

And I think you should listen now if I tell you how. Think of him as a lazy guy and me as a heroin addict who died … if that satisfies you now. Okay?

Cody,
your son …
blaah! Therapies are *not* cool!
Just saying ….
blaaah!

Letter 19

Mom,

This is me, Cody. Remember me, the screamer kid you had? I am here now.

You should practice this stuff. The presence of self in the void of thought, within the newness of amazing grace. Poetry in motion here … and more!

Calling all angels to send Mommy to a new lifestyle. Please, God, have mercy on her soul ….

Cody

A Note

⟲⟳

From Mom … To Cody..

Hi, my son Cody.

$\mathcal{M}$y life was a crapshoot most of the time. My own mom wasn't nice, meaning kind, since she isn't a "normie" at all. She is ill—not kind; you're right.

I didn't have the easiest day after you died. You suffered a substance abuse issue, while I had an abused-woman-Stockholm-syndrome with my parents. Those things both are debilitating in themselves, and these abuse syndromes created another issue for us. Nothing was ever acceptable, and with this, helplessness and abuse from my parents was tough on me too … None of that has to do with you; that death of my soul that I suffered due to them was my fault to a T. I withered in their "care" too.

I guess if nobody loves you, you yourself must take up the effort!

Mommy

Cody died once slightly at 9 a.m. on February 1, again more so on June 13 2016, and then finally and totally in May 2017 … on a Monday morning, and for this one he didn't receive anyone's help anymore. He went on to heaven's gates alone.

Letter 20

A small note …

Mom,

$\mathcal{I}$ like to think I loved you, but at the end, your love was strongest of all, as you sold your house for my sake.

Nobody you know did that. Not a single one.

The end.

Cody

Letter 21

Hi, Mom,

$\mathcal{I}$ died early in May at approximately 10.30 a.m. I wrote to you first …

… but then erased all that I had written. The message was too sad. I just wanted to be held. My stomach was empty, and my mind was full of blame for you, myself, and Maureen, and I angrily took a coke snort with more Fentanyl in it—and died.

You don't know me anymore, Mom. You walked away from me that last day I saw you … on Mother's Day!

You don't know how I suffered. You knew *only* yourself, as a child … and then you forgot it.

The me I was isn't you, you see. This is me; that is you!. We got this mixed up!

My life was entirely up to you at the end, you see, but the fights we had over drug use took a toll on you too. The dad I had wasn't there either; he never was there but in fleeting conversations over matters as sinister as punishing me. So he's not my dad for me, but you weren't up to any more of me either, and you left me alone to die.

The Dad-and-you fights were all I knew. My entire life was spent on the talks, the tests, the arguments. It was never ending. Dad didn't care—he just likes arguing—but you did. That destroyed your sanity slowly, and I suffered. The dad I had may have the most issues, but you suffered a mental hell, as the dad you have is even worse. He suffers now, and the end was so sad for me, but you suffer still every night, I know.

Ciao,
Cody,
from heaven, from now on

Letter 22

Hi, Mom,

$\mathcal{I}$'m in heaven from now on, and I watch over you, okay!
   I can't take it if you cry and wail. Be happy that I made it here and rejoice.
   Jesus says hi also; He loves you so much.

Cody

Letter 23

Mother!

I have something amazing here, a small note from hell. Guess what, it's so "hot," you wouldn't believe it. It's truly sadistic. Here it is:

> Note: From Hell
> Arguing is "fun" for us, so keep at it, and never stop!
> Argue, argue, argue, and keep putting in late hours at work, since money *is god*.
> Satan

Grrr … I think Dad took note at least!

Please *never argue again, I beg of you all!*

I "died" of arguments and madness too. I took my drugs and died; slowly I slipped away, as a sock is pulled off a foot that's asleep, and finalized anything that was left over from your marriage with Dad.

This was my exit, my way. Nobody could tell me what to do anymore. Only that sadness lingers ….

The adults have things to do, right? But I didn't quite reach that point. The mesmerizing death of a youth has gone largely unnoticed, as he didn't really contribute; he was just a kid.

What do people want me for anyway? I decided to leave it all for them to find out.

Cody

Note to Dad

I'm sorry it ended this way, Dad. I had troubles also, but I wasn't alone in this. My hobbies weren't really there anymore after a while, and you truly tried to become someone important in my life.

I also trusted you in your choices for me. I knew you cared a lot about yourself and were there for me as a dad, at some odd times when you had a chance ….

You always won in business deals, and you tried hardest of them all; you truly do still. Where you work they make a lot of money, and I was proud of that.

I loved it as you drove me around once or twice in your large car and gave me all kinds of small food portions and a few gifts to keep. I totally loved it. I wanted to be your *son*, the one you were happiest with, and I wasn't so alone at those few times, as you were with me when—I can't remember when, but a few days here and there, at least.

(and I appreciate this, *so much*)

Love,
Your son,
Cody

Letter 24

Hi, Mommy,

*W*hen we had fights, you and I weren't all there mentally, neither of us. We were often tired. You weren't high; you stayed up all night worrying or going through the bills. I'm sorry; I shouldn't have been so aggravated by your efforts to keep me safe.

The end is sooner than soon for most of us, nearing when nothing is done to help especially. But you helped and were happy always if I made it. That much I know now. When people cease to help out, they aren't real people anymore. They care only about themselves.

Cody
I loved you, Mommy!

Letter 25

Hi, Mommy,

*C*an you give this letter to my sister? She's awesome. She told me about Jesus, and she kindly told me about love and angels and such. I listened, but I didn't *believe*. I was, to put it mildly, a little bit skeptical about Jesus also; I wasn't sure ….

In the end *He* was there for me, and I said, "*Wow*, that's Mom's best friend!"

I knew you were right then, and I told *Him* I wasn't ready to leave yet. He said, "No, Son, you are coming now, and it's a bit lazy of you not to thank your mom for this, but you are to go on to heaven now."

He was sure you went to a crazy state for a while, soon after you heard that I had died alone … but *He* was there for you, you know, and wanted you to know this.

All of us die someday; to me it was so soon. I had so many thoughts that day. I wanted to fly away but kept at you, telling you I wasn't ever going to come to you again. I was sure I wasn't, and I went on ….

And here I am again, and I am writing you to let you know this: Love is eternal, and you live, love, and learn how to work again. You will find somebody who cares about you too, and he will be healthy—not sick like my own dad was. He is a really cool kid indeed. Very many moms are crying here too. They never said goodbye, but we had a hug even.

So many aren't strong enough to just walk away like you did, they tell their sons so many evil words and then leave and let go, but you never let go. You phoned somebody to go and help me; he just never wanted to come!

(He was so busy.)

I love you, Mom, and I love sister Maureen too, so much ….

I want you to know that there is a God, and he is surely a good God. He can't let you go alone much longer, so become who you are, and never fake again; truly be you.

Cody,
your loving son from heaven
PS: Today is Mother's Day again. Don't cry; rejoice, since I loved you.

Letter 26

Hi, Mommy,

$\mathcal{I}$ wanted you to know that I am well today.

You thought about me again, more than anything else, and bought a painting of a soaring eagle, standing for freedom (from drug use).

I love it.

For me it symbolizes freedom as something plain and simple, just the way I wanted it. Keep it near you, and watch me soar. With this picture you proved one thing: you love still, and every day you do cry still. I don't not see that, I know you suffered a lot. I am so, so sorry! I am.

Cody,
your *own* son ...
from heaven

Letter 27

Hi, Mom,

*C*an you please stop doubting this phenomenon, my writing this through your hands? I have one secret here, a book you never liked to finish.

This book I'll send next is a small nod from heaven to you that you are gifted. It speaks about seven levels on earth, which you already wrote about, and it tells people how to live well.

Just tell those who doubt that they are fools. They don't know you, nor did I! I doubted you too, but now I regret it. I'm so sorry; keep on writing!

Maureen, too, she has this gift also. So be happy that you two are together, and have fun at it. Most moms can't. Sometimes it's hard to be a "best pal" with your son, but you did that also! Mom, you're awesome—that's what Sister says too—so trust it now.

I wanted you to become a better mom for me at times, not to yell as I used, and not to scream at Dad who cheated, lied, and abused. Don't become that, but still, trust me when I tell you that I know now he isn't a really great dad, and be yourself.

Just be yourself. Don't doubt at all, but be.

Cody

Letter 28

Hi, Mommy,

I am happy today! I told Maureen today that she can start skateboarding. I will sit and watch, as she is soaring too. She is more free than I ever wanted to be actually. She cares, but she isn't caring too much; that is good. If you cared for me, you might have cared a bit too much, as you left all your possessions and left your houses for my sake. I think that's what you are: an angel in the making ….

Take care, Mom, and don't cry alone. Whenever you feel like it, tell me, and I'll make you laugh and smile again.

PS: I appreciate the house business so much that I am happy for you for it. You know, here in heaven they appreciated it too, as you told them to tell me that it's okay. You know how many people would do that kind of thing? No one. No one sells their beach house to cater to a guy like me who isn't always sober even for three days straight. I mean, most parents think they might, but they never actually do shit like that, and actually, you may be the only one.

Take care—I mean it.

Cody

Hi, Mom,

*M*y new parents are here! Today is a special day for us drug users who died young. We get "fostered" by heavenly angels. I got these two—here's a picture of their smiling faces—and yes, they are super nice! I think you may be the one on the left actually, but this is an older pic of you, and that one on the right—you're right, sister, she is a parent also, for me.

You know why they chose you two for me? I know, they said these two know me well enough to tell me what to do. Should I listen now even? *Yes*, I am listening to you and Maureen from now on, and you were right, a hundred times more right than any other adult I ever met. Keep at it, Mommy!

Maureen again is the sister angel for a drug-addicted teenage boy. She has it! She isn't wishy-washy but tells how it is. Don't cry; move over to the other side as your turn comes, and then we party—all right!

Lifestyles I had weren't sober or appropriate for a teenager. You know I lied too; I lied to you straight out of meanness. I wanted more drugs. I said I needed coffee or lunch money when I actually received it from Daddy dearest and you! See, you weren't a fool, but Dad thinks you were. He's so nasty!

Parents of drug abusers take a lot. They actually suffer *more* than the user does. They take on this role to become holy. They seek for God *more than* any other parent or sibling would, praying and wailing and asking for help.

That is the finest design of our God's: so that He can help them and prove that He is an okay God, He takes us out first. That way you get to live in a state of grace forever after it's over. Then you and I will party when we are meeting again, and I tell you: God's parties are *good*. They last *forever—and* they are drug free, yet we all are super high! :)

Cody

Letter 30

Hi, Mom,

*T*ell my siblings that drug use isn't always bad, but it ends badly if you aren't careful. They don't know this. If you tell a child, "Don't do drugs," they'll do it! But if you tell the truth, they'll understand better what is bad and good ….

Lying tells them it's A-OK to use as it wasn't as bad as you said. Just a hint.

Also tell them I loved them. I'm sad that I missed their teenage years too … and I will tell them also, in a subliminal way, like this: They may wake up sometimes and sense me around, feeling awful if they lie about their whereabouts, who they are with and such. I'll keep an eye on them. I don't want them to die or suffer either. Trust in me.

I care,
Cody

Letter 31

Hi, Mom,

$\mathcal{I}$ was sleeping well last night. I went well past 7 a.m.! I think you did as well ….

Here we have what they call sleep-induced meditative practices. They work well for addicts. We dream a lot when we rest. (That's why I lay in bed all day too! I'm sure you get it.) I dream of a small place for you, but it isn't a large hut or anything; it's a small cave sort of a place where you can dream and write. What do you say? I think that would be awesome, right?

I think you are a mom through and through, Mommy. I loved you *so much*, you see, that I'm still writing here, from heaven. (Most kids, don't you know, they go out and see different things here. It's awesome here, you see—like paradise times ten, at least!)

I still loved you after you sent me away. And I still *am* loving you. I wish you could see this so well that you wouldn't cry at night so much.

Cody,
your *son* in heaven

Letter 32

Hi, Mom,

$\mathcal{T}$oday is a special day again here, as you have a cabin where you can sit and write! I arranged it; I'm sure I did! I couldn't face the sadness on your face when you cried over your lost lair on the California coastline, lost for my sake! I am sad also, but at the end, variation is key. So don't be sad and look outside.

Isn't it a beautiful place?

It has the best ever sunshine and sea, with bald eagles—and even whales out there, that you can see right off your porch. But you are always very sad now. Just think about me and how I never get to "use" again.

Now that brings a hint of a smile to your face, doesn't it?

I knew it! Now you laugh even a bit, "No more using drugs there." Don't you use any drugs, Mommy, ever (but weed is okay sometimes, I think).

Your *son in heaven* …,
Cody, who died at nineteen … of *drug use*

Letter 33

Hi, Mom,

*L*oving you is like a summer's breeze. It cools my essence and brings a small shiver. A small little mommy like you took me alone to *Paris*, even *Tokyo*; we went to Bangkok in *Thailand* together and to *Morocco!* And we got to hike the mountains into a Lahu village and see elephants, giraffes, crocodiles, and even the real panda bear! And even something like a cat bear.

Wow, Mom! How did you dare, alone, with two little kids in tow? I was scared sometimes to even go to school alone! I was more scared than most, actually. See, my dad's side has generational afflictions such as anxiety; you didn't get this at all!

You didn't even know what general anxiety disorder means, as you just *are*. I wish I was more like you, one of those little Scandinavians who could.

Cody

Hi, Mom, down there on earth!

$\mathcal{I}$'m having a blast today, I see you writing these letters again, but having a mom like yourself can be sometimes challenging. This time now I appreciate it, but then, as you spoke about God and Jesus all the time—well, not truly enough!!

If a "new turn on earth" or such should be awarded, I could now go to school and become a lawyer for you. I think you needed a truly dedicated one instead of what you got!

Dad wasn't always very straightforward with you, and he was at times a very nasty piece of work. He can't get enough of anybody's misery, you see, as that's his power on earth.

You didn't care actually too much. You just got stressed around his essence, since you only wanted to live in peace.

All you need now is to have something to share with that sister of mine, the essence of mine … a laid-back loving soul … and that dad, who cleverly conned you always, can't trust you at all, because you never lie!

He can't, because he isn't capable of anything like this, nor is he able to be imagining honesty, as he has never experienced it for himself at all!

Don't ever care that he left you to cry alone after I died. That's just what that kind of person does.

Bye,
Cody
(I love you, Mom!)

Letter 35

Hi, Mom,

$\mathcal{W}$ hat day is it today? Oh, it's Maureen's B-day!! Tell her I said hi, and ask her to leave these sadistic ideas of "success via wealth" behind today!

I am sure she'll understand what you mean if you only tell her this: I have never had anything at all, and she … has always had a lot!

Most of my money came from stealing, lying, and being sneaky—to obtain some cash flow at least—but you, Mom, never were stingy. If you had anything at all, you spent it on *us kids*.

The work you do today, Mommy, has three items God smiles about. Helping poor people is good, number one; helping addicted youth is good, number two; and helping people see me as I truly am is good, number three! I truly appreciate you today, Mom! God is good, and trust what He says now. You will *not die alone*, Mom. He has something in store for you too!

Loving others with all your heart is your deal, and that's what counts.

I love you, Mommy, and please trust in me when I say this now. You aren't going to "die alone"—no way!

Cody

Letter 36

Hi, Mommy,

$\mathcal{I}$ wasn't always nice either, to you or to Maureen. Mom, I know this.

I know today you that don't care about these past "small things" that I was into, but I do! I truly do care, I'm so sorry, Mom. I don't know how I thought I would survive all the drug use, stealing, and lying to you and Maureen. I never truly had a "plan B": I thought, *Maybe someday I'll just stop using*. That didn't catch up with me; dying alone did before you got to me … so don't allow yourself to argue with anybody any longer (it's *not* worth it). Thousands of arguments came and went; nothing was achieved except extremely bad, sad, and painful memories, for all three of us. It's *not* worth arguing with anyone at all.

Just leave, and leave all bad people from your life *right now!*

Cody,

your son who died at merely nineteen, too early not, but too soon for you and Maureen! And also for their sake who take a dose too many, please consider that they suffer more than you can imagine! (So don't be sad, but breathe, and make your chilli bowls—they will be amazing!)

PS: I want you to be *happy*, Mommy, I truly do. I don't want you to cry alone every single day. It's so sad. So sad to watch from over on this side too. The angels weep for you too—and they do care. Sorry, Mom—I mean it!

And super thanks for being my mother, Mommy. I truly will be a good guardian angel of mercy and grace for you every single day for the rest of your life. I promise.

Letter 37

Hi, Mom,

$\mathcal{I}$ have news! God sent me this note:

"Parents who argue can't know what it does to a child. The hell is on every single day. Parents who co-parent can't argue, or else it isn't co-parenting; instead, it's abusive to all those involved. Your child's dad was a sales guy, his mom a stay-at-home mother for most of his life. The dad wasn't thinking about this child much, but now he has some ideas of what he could perhaps have done. That makes Cody smile, as you still 'won' the games his dad was playing. Now Dad has to think again before he takes another wife!"

"He truly shouldn't remarry, but now he may do it, and also—he truly has to wonder whether he still can handle Claudia. She's somewhat like a movie star. She even said once, to your child, Cody, "Get out, get of here right now!" We think she was drinking … as she yelled at him drunk and threw her handbags after him. Thus he left.

"And with some tears streaming down on his slight cheeks he walked alone at night all the way downtown, seeking for a heroin dose to end his life—while his dad only looked on."

Mom, I had that memory in my head as I died alone: his stare, her screaming at me with all her might, and me leaving their apartment alone …

Luckily I gave *you* a call, and you talked me out of it. I went to a friend's house to talk instead of killing myself out of spite.

Still, that night wasn't yet where the most devastating blow came to me. That came later on when you, Mom, left me alone that day (for One day!) … and that's when I "did the deed" of a life-changing fentanyl dosing …

Cody,
your son in heaven now …

PS: I loved you, Mom.
I'm so sorry ….

Letter 38

Hi, Mom,

*T*hat last memory was devastating, but now I'm okay.

I seek for you everywhere, and I find out here who you truly were before we met! You were a true dancer, a jazz dancer to boot, and really limber, beautiful, and always smiling. You looked like a small movie starlet from the 'sixties. I think you knew; boys were circling you all the time, I think, I counted at least ten who truly liked you (at a time), and then you chose me to come to this world. Thanks!

I loved it.

(We always had fun together, never too much sorrow and yelling like at Dad's houses.) I think you were the best mom ever. My friends loved you too … but they never knew that *I* had the coolest mom. I never introduced them to you! I should have!

Mom, just one more thing: I loved you. You know this, right? And I want to make sure you knew, but you did doubt. Because my stepmom was a monster to me always, you encouraged me to still seek for my dad's arms too, but I refused. He wasn't a dad to me, truly; he was just a pay-pal with an attitude as bad as his heart.

Bye for now,
Cody

Letter 39

Mom,

$\mathcal{I}$ want to tell you something now. I loved you and Maureen, but I *hated* Valeriane, Dad;s second wife.

She's a true a**hole. Truly, very well, she can't be that bad, but Dad had her primed to hate you and me. I have never been so sad as when she was tormenting me—Maureen also at times, but mostly me.

I can't believe an adult woman would be so conniving!

How about me then? I was a two-year-old kid when it started, and it lasted for eleven years! I nearly collapsed under it all. I started using drugs more and more, and she escalated, obviously to prove to you that she knew how bad you were, and so me too—and it's all *wrong*.

Her sense of self was all cash flow–based. That's why she married Dad, so you know, and she got it. That is, she got it and she lost it as soon as the next tail came to sight (and the next, and then even the next, and so on …), but ultimately she isn't so bad anymore. She has learned some things in life.

These things at least, I presume: first, that money doesn't buy happiness, but truthfulness doesn't always either, Mom (you don't need to yell at Maureen, as the truth is there also—and all this, by the way, she knows; she just doesn't care so much. After all, she's still accepted there). But I left it all behind in one swift weekend of drug use, and that's also Valeriane's fault. For too, too many years she abused me, a little kid, until I crumbled at last and was a *drug addict!*

Now she truly has an *excuse* to hate me ….

That's all for today,

Cody,

who died at nineteen alone in his suite … officially due to Fentanyl, but actually due to early child abuse by adults who didn't give a small-scale rat's ass about him—at all!

Mom,

$\mathcal{T}$oday is a celebration day.

You just got out! I am seeing you embarking to Mexico (too soon), but that's so cool. I wish I could be there for you; I know you are alone, but still.

You are going on this trip for the first time in two years to seek for happiness somewhere. If there is anyone who is nice to you, smile at least. You can (I don't mind, since you think I would, because I died and you didn't become my hero that night to save me), and you never thought I'd say this, but yes—I want you to remember me always happy.

That's where I went, to become happier at least, and not so sad as you last saw me. I send pictures! (I know how; heaven has many avenues.)

And I'm so sorry by the way about my friend Thomas. He has a "problem"—not as bad as mine, but still.

You know those kids, they aren't communicative when they use drugs, but they are so kind when they aren't using, so you shouldn't be arguing with yourself anymore about whether you said something to become a "pest," the way you always think you do!

It's not true. You *are not* a pest, and they all also said it. All my friends know you're okay. It's all their drug use that takes their attention away from anybody, even their own mothers, so why not you, as you are only some friend's mom after all.

(But you *are* the coolest—or that's *my* opinion at least.)

Cody

Letter 41

Hi, Mommy,

$\mathcal{I}$ have some good news today!

I am at the heavenly college and starting to study today. Aren't you happy for me? I actually will start tomorrow, as in heaven it's today ;), any day all day long, and I study artistic penciling—and it's fun! I like it.

These things are valued here, craftsmanship, artistic endeavors, and also prayers to God. Constantly we praise Him and rejoice in His presence!

I know you are wondering about me a lot. I *have* things to do here in heaven; we don't just sit and reminisce about life. We are living every "day" here in heaven to the fullest, and we do stuff: we visit others, we sing, we rejoice—oh, I already mentioned that, but there is something else that is new to you. We also go to school, and then guess what!

We teach someone else there on earth how to as well, so first I learn how to draw these letters so perfectly, and then somebody on earth realizes how it's done, through me helping them in such a way that they think they realized it themselves. That's how angels help humans all the time: they suddenly seem to think, "Ha, that's a cool design I could use!" And I was "it" for that to happen! Do you get it?

All beauty stems from heaven, so you see, wherever you seek for beauty, there you see the work of thousands of angels first.

Your son, Cody,
from heaven's college of
printing nice!

Letter 42

Hi, Mom,

$\mathcal{I}$ graduated! I am done at heaven's school of printing nice now, and I move on. It was fun, but now it's done and over with. I was good at it and shone like the brightest student that I would have been, should anybody have cared for me when I was a child. They didn't see me shine at school, as you and Dad fought all the time, and I started to care less and less, as nobody paid any attention to me.

I was a silent kid and took to my room and played video games (which I was *really* good at by the way!). But nobody saw me as I am: a brilliant math head instead of a loser like you and Dad were. I was kind and sensitive, a good athlete and wise beyond my years.

Even at seven or eight years old I taught you truth and universal deep stuff! from the backseat of your car. Do you remember, Mommy?

I was the smartest kid; the most sensitive, kind kid; and the too-tough-on-myself kid also, since nobody did see me!

I am sad now to write this, but you and Dad should never have married. You see, you're too kind, and he isn't kind but an extremely hard worker. You should have married a millionaire, and he shouldn't ….

Mom, also—

I wanted to say this about you.

I loved you, and did you know this?

I want you to be sure that you know this well. I had no one else! I had no other relatives left but you, and when you turned your back on me that night, I wasn't prepared to go on … *alone* yet. I was just a kid, a lonesome kid, not yet an adult at all!

I loved you, and it hurt me so badly, and I died as a result of turning away from you, and your becoming hurt and sad so that you started also turning away from me at the end.

Mom, you sent me to heaven.

I loved you,
your son who is still in your admiration,
Cody

Letter 43

Hi, Mom,

$\mathcal{I}$'m hoping you're well; you look better today!

Are you eating now? I always have to ask, since you juiced and health-smoothie'd me to death, haha ….

I hope all you wellness freaks are okay to take a break now and there, since it's a short life, and a lot of good food is out there!

I loved eating a lot.

I would have loved to have more food in my life. I relive only a few great things, but meals together were the greatest times I remember fondly!

You cook quite well already, Mom, and I actually appreciated it a lot when you did cook for me. I did seek to help out sometimes, even financially at the end, and you received it graciously. Thank you, Mommy, for having me. I was your number one, right? I think you loved me a lot, without knowing it. I think you did, as you did a lot for me every day.

You taught me how to drive, how to work, and how to be very independent of people's thoughts and opinions, that kind of stuff. But you didn't tell me how to not be afraid. You were afraid of Dad and thousands of others too —and that destroyed you. You didn't want to fight, but that guy isn't all about giving his money away, so thanks, Mom, for nothing, for fighting him over it.

I hope you're wiser now and ask for nothing from those folks; they love their cash. It's impossible and dangerous to approach such a thing. They don't realize, but they do argue a lot.

Mom, one other thing: take care now, okay? Don't be so hard on yourself, and be. Just be yourself; I died for this, you know.

Your son, Cody,
from heaven

Letter 44

Hi, Mommy,

*T*oday is Tuesday, right? This day is a wonderful day to sleep in and enjoy life. The fluffy pillows, the view—perfect. I think you'd like to work a little less and *be* a bit more, right? I think I can help.

Remember how I sent you notes on my cell phone? I sent things like "Hi" or "Thanks" or something short like that, and you went on and on. Just text short messages from now on; that saves time! Also, don't run or anything—though it truly saves time if you do, as you don't have to go anywhere to work out … and also, it's free.

Also, don't think so much; it's an energy-wasting activity. I think very little nowadays, I flow about, and things get done anyway, without *any* thought whatsoever, since here we just are. We fall into love all the time also (giggles here), as we are In Love always, but we fall into it too, I tell you why … here.

> *I love you, you love me …*
> *We're a happy family … etc.*

You know that Barney song! Guess who wrote it: me! I had my fingers in the play when it came about, and then I was born to sing it … well, it's true, I loved it, right?

My time is up; I've got to go. We have an assembly with Jesus. He's taking us hiking … so we can experience His presence where there are gaps to be filled in and experiences we didn't get enough of on earth.

Bye now. I'll tell you later how it was.

Cody, "The Hiker of the God Sent Hills"

Letter 45

Mom to Cody, on May 15th …

*W*hen I fought with Dad, I didn't mean it. I was just worried he was not truly there for us. He wasn't, and … I was right.

———

When I fought with the doctor who prescribed you more pills, about you and how young you were to take Percocet or such … I wasn't truly meaning it.

I was just frustrated that nothing was done. And I wasn't asking for more than a care place that you could be at sometimes.

Something that would work! (instead of a rehab). I am so sorry. I was worried sick.

———

When I fought with the administrators at a care facility, I wasn't truly sad with them. I was just angry that they didn't offer anything suitable for an intelligent young man who couldn't care less about these groups and such—

or with some little counselor's suggestions on breathing, when my son struggles with life and death and has nothing to live for anymore.

Truly, I am so angry, even today, since I still can't know what killed you exactly.

I hope it wasn't us!

The anger I held toward you too, I think that was also anger toward myself mainly, as I was so angry toward your dad, *and* due to an issue within me. How worried I was and scared. How little I felt after you went away, as nobody phoned me, and nobody came by either. Nobody even knew that I was your mom and should be notified!

I wasn't mentioned in the paperwork, I who carried you on my hip for four years straight after you were born and then sat never farther than two feet away from you typically for over seventeen years. I was there for the soccer, for the doctor's appointments. I even was there and drove you to the police station after your small scrap with the law, and I was the one teaching you how to pray too.

So why was no one there for me after you died? I was lying alone in my apartment for three to four months before I finally got up—and the only person then who even cared to listen to me was this young waitress who was working at a coffee shop nearby. We shared a few words here and there. Why wasn't anybody else there for me after you were taken off this world?

Mom

Letter 46

Hi, Mom,

$\mathcal{I}$ am feeling loved. I am happy and healthy, I fly ….

Who cares if I die now? I am taking pills and I am floating and millions of small "tingles" are dancing around. I smile and breathe less and less. It's seven a.m. on Monday; where am I?

Lovely, lovely Mom, I love you so. Where are you? Aren't you home? I remember you were cooking something good; was it porridge with jam? I am happy and light—I took fentanyl pills; they truly are the thing to do if you want to die swiftly and lightly ….

Mommy, don't cry out loud like that. It's over … well, for me it is, but you seem sad. Why are you screaming?

Mom, can't you hear me? *Mom—Mom!*

Cody,
from heaven's doorways ….

Letter 47

Hi, Mommy,

I am a "Hiker of the God Sent Hills" now. I was there for a million and a half years, and now I'm back. We saw dinosaurs; angels came too, and so on. We saw fish walking on two feet and other cool stuff. You won't believe what I'll send you tomorrow; just wait! I'll send you a turtleneck sweater and hiking boots! I promise … and then we go! Okay?

I come with you and guide you up to a slope of never-ending bliss and back, safe and exhausted. This hill is in Mexico, so better to be prepared with cool water and some sunscreen. I'm so in love. I loved you, and now I love this. Angels have *fun* always, and they love their subjects, just like I you.

… one two three one two three …

Bye, Mom. I hope you love the boots I will choose tomorrow for your hiking career ….

Same

Letter 48

Hi, Mom,

$\mathcal{I}$ wanted you to be okay from now on, and I wasn't sure what to say anymore, as you still whine here. I know, it's sad. Yada yada yada … and so on.

How about this, a funny face or a clown? What about this, a fun flower or the rest of a muffin that I spared, or what about this—a birthday cake! You didn't get those; I didn't either, but just wait. God says something now: "Happy Birthday to You … Happy Birthday to You … Happy Birthday, dear Mom … Happy Birthday to You!" Yay!

Okay, happier? Well wishes to sis too, as her birthdays were parties, but never yours or mine; we just dropped this habit on earth somehow—I guess since we "adults" don't need birthdays or any other holiday celebrations either. Wrong; we all need them. Appreciation isn't exactly super common, so the day is all about that.

And by the way, your own mother isn't well, as she celebrates her and her husband's birthdays but not ours or yours! She has an issue—envy, I presume—and she's stingy too, very stingy, to others, not toward herself!

How about this? Next year on my birthday you ask Maureen to join you in singing "Happy Birthday" to me, and then I'll be happy here in heaven. These celebrations *must* be observed from now on; I don't take no for an answer.

Cody,
nineteen forever—yes!

PS: My birthdays are happiest, as now I have them every single day, and they are awesome, very well planned; huge gifts are given and a lot of cake! "Boo" to you for not celebrating me when I was there, okay!

All this *madness* of not celebrating birthdays began when your dad's health got worse. Okay, so you had a lot on the go, I know. I think they stopped celebrating you at age eight or nine already, so you thought that was the age when we should stop too. I think they feel now that you aren't there for them at all. No—but that's right! *Neither were they!* So don't stress; just celebrate with Maureen, and let it go ….

Letter 49

Mom to Cody in heaven!

Where are you?

Is everything okay? How is it there, Cody? How are you?

————————

I loved my boy, and he was most often found with me. Alone or together, we were an item, to be found text messaging or phoning each other at least twice a day.

We had a "soul connect" somehow. I understood him, and he me. Nobody like that has ever existed for me, and it took over thirteen months for me to recuperate enough to leave the house properly to go for a longer walk even. As he died I was stunned; *shock* isn't a strong enough of a word for what I went through. I could be seen stumbling along, taking turns with my vehicle, for a while not knowing where I went or why.

I am in therapy currently for trauma, they say. He died in an accident in a sense, but I knew he would die, and nobody listened to me! He had "suicidal ideations," they say, and I know it, as he talked often about it. I knew that had he been among others, he could have survived! But since he was left alone, there was no chance at all, as I was rendered powerless.

I was still helping him but suddenly was entirely powerless over some of those others who went on and rented him a place to live, where he took his last doses of fentanyl and died. To die was his ultimate way to leave off of all pain and sadness. I was so against this …. He was so sad that it breaks my heart, and I still see his face, with tears on his cheeks when he tells me how much pain he had inside.

Anger isn't the issue for me anymore. It's more sadness. I'm alone and sad and kind, but so alone.

Sorry, Cody, for all that I have done wrong toward you. Don't be mean or angry in heaven, but recall me, and think about me some days, as I am alone now and will be for most of my life from now on, I know.

Mom

Letter 50

Mom to Cody

$\mathcal{I}$ slept well last night, Cody. I wasn't sure if you would call me up (in a dream) or not, but I slept through it all. Where are you? I wish I could see you ….

———————

My son died last year of a combination of fentanyl, Xanax, and cocaine, all mixed up at the same time. His heart couldn't take it. He was dead when he was found at eleven the next morning. My ex-husband found him and yelled and screamed as he phoned.

I am alone now. I always thought I would remarry, but I didn't. So aloneness isn't really what I planned for in life ….

Letter 51

Hi, Mom,

$\mathcal{I}$'m home. I came here yesterday evening. It's fantastic; I love it.

I loved you like I love a sunrise, and I love you still.

Don't cry, please. I took some drugs and died—sorry! I am so sorry, Mommy. Please don't cry; it hurts me here to see you suffering.

I have a friend here in heaven. His name is Charles (he arrived yesterday also). He's a drug user, and we have a lot in common. We both had abuse at home, but we were smart and sensitive people, and you know what? He says hello. He says abuse created this, and you shouldn't blame yourself alone.

Hi, Mom (I just wanted to say this again). We said these things so often without a worry in the world at times. We took our chances and traveled, recall? I went to Mexico and Hawaii several times even with you. That was *fun!*

I loved you and Maureen. You were my family!

Tell Maureen I said hi … Cody.

Letter 52

Mom,

$\mathcal{I}$ am happy too today. We have a party coming up. Jesus's birthday is nearing. He's a cool kid, that Jesus, just like you told me. He can't wait to meet you face to face someday.

Love,
Cody,
from heaven

Letter 53

Hi, Mom,

I'm happy for you. Today you don't need to be alone! (You are going to a workshop for accountants!)

I truly *hate* when you sit alone in your small apartment at home; that's so sad! I wish you'd never met Dad, actually I do! I think Dad hasn't got a lot going for himself but you take the brunt end of that stick for yourself.

Why?

Now stop that and get going! Get to work, you lazy little ... okay, well, you know who that is! (Dad to all people in this world) ... but it should help!

Cody,
your son from heaven

Letter 54

From Cody:

$\mathcal{I}$ loved you like a son would, and I cherished you ….

We laughed and cried together … and we understood that it wasn't to be ….

How did we know? I don't understand this, but heaven is real, so don't despair, Mommy. I am here ….

Tell Maureen to read Scriptures. Ecclesiastes 11 is good! Live on. Say nothing to anyone about these letters now, but be okay that this is *gone by and over with* … so less is more, okay?

My mom's son,
Cody … aka the best son ever
♥ … in heaven from now on ….

Letter 55

A poem from heaven (by Cody) …

If you had talked of my God
as I have talked about you,
you could have saved me.
~~
If you had talked
about me the way I now share about
you, you could have
saved me.
~~
if you could see how I love you,
I could shine a light at your face,
and you would love me back, as
a star I have for
you.
~~
"I have a star to give to
every child," says God
and gives me one.
The star is you,
Mommy.
~~~

—Cody, your son in heaven now

A Poem

To Cody …

*O*ut beyond ideas of wrongdoing and right doing there is a field.
I'll meet you there. When the soul lies down in that grass the world is too full to talk about.

—Rumi

A Poem

By Mom to Cody …

He was the kindest man walking on this earth,
wise beyond his young years.
He suffered, and
he learned fast to hold on tight
to his emotions, and to be silent,
while listening and reflecting,
but never speaking aloud
about how sad he often felt.

He was a special poet
of lifestyles,
and he knew how to live well!
As he never said a bad word,
never cursed or yelled,
now he is a brightest star in heaven
where he came from, the day
he was born.

And he shines his wisdom on us, as this name,
Cody, is a son of wealth ….
But that truly wasn't your share, Cody.
The wealth was there for you, but never given to you to enjoy.
I'm so sorry
you died young and poor.

—Mom

A Poem

The soul has been given its own ears to hear things, mind does not understand.

—Rumi

Hi, Mom,

I tried to call you last night. I was sad. I was alone.
You and Dad are fighting, always fighting ….
I am taking drugs this weekend to forget it all …

*j*ust like you do when you drink some days. I am not a bad boy or anything. I'm just sad that you fought my entire life …. I wanted to be free of this shit, yeah, all of it ….

I am going home now and taking my drugs and going to bed ….

Bye for
… now,
Cody, aka
Cody, your son
(That morning he was found dead)

Letter 57

Hi, Mom,

I'm floating …. This is strange. I woke up, and you weren't there. I picked up my phone, and there wasn't anything on it. I remembered that those guys I met (and adored) took my better one, with the SIM card intact, and I now only have this old wreck of a phone with a busted screen on it. I'm so sorry.

I took a lot of drugs last night, but I feel strange.

It's as if I am floating!

Cody …

PS: You know what? I think I died last night—sigh …. All I wanted was for you to be happy with me. I guess I failed a lot!

Letter 58

Mom—Mom!

$\mathcal{W}$here r you?—Mom!
  Cody
  (I miss you, Mom ….)

at approximately nine p.m. the following Friday

Mom!

I'm floating alone in an abyss. I can't see anybody here at all ….
  I'm all alone.
  Mom! Mom!
  Are you there? Mom?

A Note

from Cody's mommy

Three years ago on this date in May, Cody was found "unresponsive" in his own bed at eleven a.m. or so.

He wasn't breathing anymore, but he was still warm, and his body was taken away swiftly to the morgue without any further ado.

My life ended right there… he says. My life is *over* now. Period. †

A Note

by Cody's mom

On a May day as sunny as could be … this world lost the kindest of hearts. A man who was to be a true champion of the poor, the lost.

My son, Cody—and all of a sudden I heard his dad screaming in my ear through his cell phone, "They're taking him away! They're taking him!"—and he left the scene …

God, let him rest in peace … just let Cody now rest in peace!

A Note

from Mom to Cody's dad

I text him back this:

_____ Just a blank line, meaning: I have nothing more to say.

I collapse on the floor and cry ... then my fingers start dialing the number of a friend, to take me in to see our family doctor to get something to carry me through all this. I receive pills, and I'm numb for several weeks on end.

When I finally gave them up, the pain was unimaginable. My loving son was gone for good. This pain feels like a cannon shot through my heart and soul, and the emptiness makes me cringe every second of the day. The agony and pain merge into a hollowness in my gut the size of that cannonball.

He's dead? Really? I'm not sure, somehow. I feel his presence, but he isn't there. I fear I did it somehow to him. Was it me or you? Who did this?

Aren't we the parents of this child? *We are responsible and guilty, and I am ashamed* of myself. Why didn't I go and check on Cody when I felt Jesus Himself calling my name, for his sake! Isn't this your son too, though? Where were you in all this?

I was such a fool ... to trust you instead.

Mother of Cody

: (

Letter 60

Hi, Mom,

I'm good, how are you? I'm in heaven, you see … and it's fabulous. Very nice indeed.

I have friends here, and I am not alone anymore. Why don't you say also that you need some friends? Why don't you tell them you're a Christian, so you can get the *right* friends for you? I think you should.

More and more, tell this truth all over the place: God cares about all of us … He truly does.

And since Christians don't let go of each other, and they do care too, right? So they are the friends for you!

Bye for now, Mommy.

I'm going to bed early tonight! :)

Cody,
your son in heaven

Letter 61

Epigraph … to Cody,

I loved you a lot—

Mommy

A Poem

The cure for pain is in the pain.

—Rumi

Letter 62

Hi, Mom,

*T*oday I am serious about something … working.

Aren't you the laziest person alive? No, you aren't. Dad is.

Dad is *so lazy that all he does* is gamble and play. He never works at all. He has all the toys too, and then some. And his partner isn't much better. She "works," as in she presents herself at the office and smiles, but that's it; she isn't capable of much else at all!

You were. You worked day and night many days; at night you wrote reports for clients, and during the days, you were busy with us kids.

I appreciate this today, I was too small to see the tired dark circles under your eyes before this happened, and I thought you napped due to exhaustion from caring for us, so I played in my bedroom to give you space.

You worked, at nights mostly, for many years, so you could be with us without using nannies, being all by yourself during the days, and working nights too. I appreciate this. I think Dad should have learned something by now, but he hasn't. He still just plays games with people and has fun with it. He's still "in business," in his mind at least, and he is very "important" to someone who makes money off him.

And he isn't kind. He still "kills" my little brother too. If he doesn't come to his senses soon, as he's bullied so much at school now that he isn't fine anymore. Dad doesn't see that, because he's a bully himself. He think it's fun to bully people, as in "What's wrong with that?" He's amused at their agonies and says to himself this as well: "Just get a grip on yourself!"

Whoa!

How about that, Mommy. Can't you see? Why did you love this man? I'm just asking ….
?????

I think he was just like your mother—all in all, a truly self-centered person, more like a demon-possessed adult might be. Yeah, that's right, a narcissistic, demon-possessed adult isn't *fun* to be with. I salute you for divorcing him early on. You shouldn't have stayed in California though, as it was too nearby. They tend to linger; you see, they want you "dead or alive." And if you leave them, there's hell to pay; that's how their demon whispers into their ear that you are so stupid that they can't believe it … and so annoying and so sinister to me that they want you_*back* in their lives, *now*. See—it makes no sense!

They aren't crazy but just truly deranged!

I think you know what I mean by these words now: "Stay away for good."

And *if* you ever think about them, just think about a lazy guy and a stupid, angry stay-at-home mom instead, okay?

Bye,
your loving son,
Cody, from heaven

Life in the Spirit

So now there is no condemnation for those who belong to Christ …. And because you belong to him, the power of the life-giving Spirit has freed you from the power of sin that leads to death …. God … sent his own Son in a body like the bodies we sinners have. And in that body God declared an end to sin … by giving his Son as a sacrifice for our sins. (Romans 8:1–3 NLT)

Letter 63

Hi, Mom,

$\mathcal{T}$oday is a celebration of senses. I'll explain.

 We can't live without them, so we need to rejoice in them,

 Why don't you buy some salves of lavender, some wine and chocolate, and also fresh cut flowers?

Ciao,

from the very Italian part of heaven today …

your son Cody,

in heaven from *now* … on …

Letter 64

I love Italians. They say "Ciao bella" to you, Mom.

*A*ll men tell you all kinds of silly stuff, so enjoy your wines and cheeses now (as you *still* are alive! Be merry. And love, okay? I love you always!).

Amore mia ….

Ciao,
from Cody
who is still in the Italian part of heaven, as it's so swell ….

Letter 65

Hi, Mom,

Tomorrow, we finally finish these letters.

I am as sad (not) as you are … ;) but let's just run with it ….

So what have you learned? I think you know by now my stance, that you aren't really solely responsible, as drug addicts die frequently, and nobody can stop them (except the police, fire brigade, and Satan himself). But we aren't friends with them, so that's all.

So what now, you seem to ask frequently nowadays? *What now?*

After a million tears shed, a small amount of weight gained, and a lot of friends and relatives banished … what *now?*

I know: perhaps try to think like this:

If you were to do something that doesn't require a lot, like writing, or at least sleeping alone and writing soon after?

Could you?

I think that would suit you (you lazy bum … :)), and we could always make amends with your parents, who have a small condo. So perhaps that's it for you or …?

Sure, it's hard … but not as hard as standing all day at the checkout bagging, or cleaning houses, so okay?

I'm for it, and I am sending a small note to God right now to please let you write alone, and travel, and be okay …

Ciao ciao

Mommy, from Cody

(who's alone seeking for some mercy and grace for Mommy, who is a complete washout by now)

Letter 66

Hi, Mommy,

$\mathcal{I}$ have "arrived" today.

I had a "review" with Jesus, and He told me to talk to you. He says you are okay.

I am very happy for you. (I worked *hard* for your soul, but today, you let be … okay.) I'm so proud of you, Mom! I think you are through this. Maureen's and Cody's fates have been sealed now. By your deeds alone, Mommy, you brought us home … with God Almighty.

Thanks, Mommy!

You are so good at this,

Cody,
your son who
is in heaven *now*

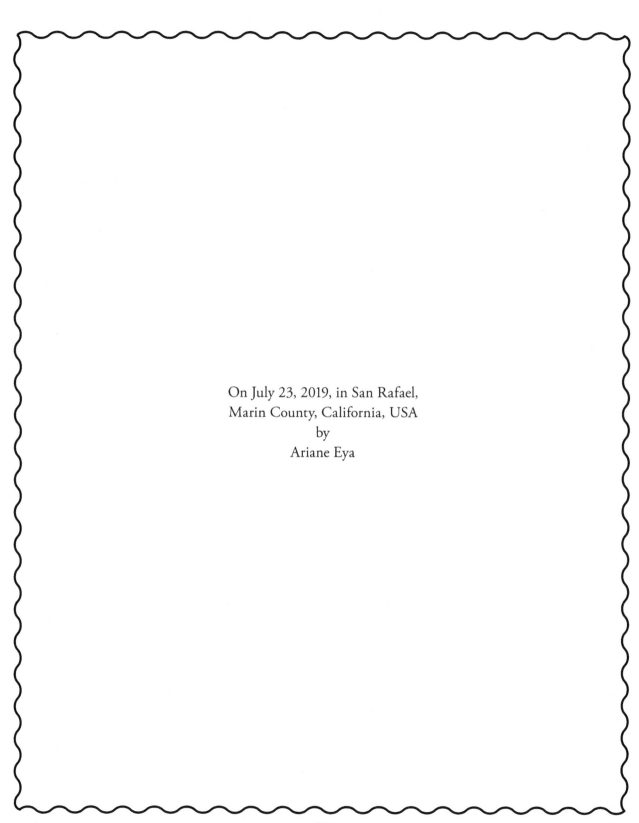

On July 23, 2019, in San Rafael,
Marin County, California, USA
by
Ariane Eya

Sources:

Centres for Disease Control and Prevention, National Centre for Health Statistics, Government of Canada:
https://health-infobase.canada.ca/datalab/national-surveillance-opioid-mortality.html#AORD

"Opioid-related harms and deaths in Canada" Government of Canada:
https://www.canada.ca/en/health-canada/services/substance-use/problematic-prescription-drug-use/opioids/data-surveillance-research/harms-deaths.html

"Accident Statistics": International Civil Aviation Organization (ICAO), a UN specialized agency:https://www.icao.int/safety/iStars/Pages/Accident-Statistics.aspx

"Casualties Graph,"Bureau of Aircraft Accidents Archives, Geneva, Switzerland:
http://baaa-acro.com/casualities-graph?created[min]=2010-01-01&created[max]=2019-12-31

"US drug overdose deaths fell slightly in 2018," by Ben Tinker, Jacqueline Howard and Jamie Gumbrecht, CNN, July 17, 2019:
https://www.cnn.com/2019/07/17/health/drug-overdose-deaths-2018-bn/index.html

About the Author

$\mathscr{A}$riane Eya, a first time author who lost her son due to a Fentanyl poisoning in early 2017 writes an emotional account for Cody and all the thousands of teens who struggle with this epidemic of suicide by drugs.

Printed in the United States
By Bookmasters